Ardency

The Tale of My Love

BookSquirrel Publications

BookSquirrel Publication

Mahadev Totala Nager, Indore (M.P),452001
Regd Under MSME
Website: *www.booksquirrelpublication.com*

"Ardency- The tale of my love"

By: Kumari Jyotsna, Atharva Bhoyarkar and Shivangi Gupta

ISBN: 978-93-89923-05-6

English & Hindi Anthology 1st Edition

Book Formatting: Mr_Ash

Cover Design: Ronak Chavda

Price: INR 199

<u>ACKNOWLEDGEMENT</u>

The completion of this anthology wouldn't have

Been possible without the cooperation of all co-

Authors, who have put their hard work and efforts

For the success of this Anthology.

A big thanks to Kumari Jyotsna, Shivangi Gupta and Atharva Bhoyarkar,

The compiler and editor who Devoted a lot of time and completed the work with full diligence.

Huge thanks to our publication team BOOK SQUIRREL PUBLICATION

Above all, big thanks to our families, friends and

All our supporters for their immense blessings and support.

It won't be possible without our Parents love and trust in us.

<u>DISCLAIMER</u>

This anthology is a work of fiction. The compilers

Have tried to make sure that all the write-ups in

This book is original and plagiarism free.

All the write-ups in this book are unique and

Belong solely to the respective Co-Authors.

In any case of plagiarism detection neither the

Publishing house nor the compilers are to be held responsible.

The sole responsibility of the write-ups are on the

Respective co-author.

Kumari Jyotsna

Basically from Bihar, Residing in Delhi is a girl named Kumari Jyotsna. She did hergraduation from Hansraj College, Delhi University and is a civil aspiring. She loves to portray her emotions and thoughts on the Paper in the form of poems. She is fond of reading books. She is a mox. Her nature of living vivaciously and keep dreaming in and wanna makes her fall in love with herself, yep! She is a bit self-obsessed.

<u>The One</u>

It was like any other days,
She started her life,
Determined to shine like sun rays
Called her parents, attended the lab,
With so many queries open on her tab.
Chirping like birds, flying like butterfly
Everything was going good,
Same routine, same mood.
The moment she sat beside the "one"
What!! Her heart pounds
Why not, she just heard,
World's best sound.
Today sun shouldn't set
Something is going to happen
Really beautiful if not so great.
She started creating a world in her mind,
Where there will be sharing of pleasure and sadness,
Although all this was only her madness.
Will walk together,
Till we achieve everything
And all height.
The world for her wasn't same anymore,
Like all the happiness in the world at her door.
Sky is more blue and leaves more green,
Her face and hairs has entirely disparate sheen.
Will be together day and night.
And much more was in her dream,
How about a day with anice-cream
Was all it her fault or the "one" sitting next.
Perhaps this time no one was wrong.
Yeah! This was life's another song.
To tell all the stuff going in the mind,
She looked her side, searched....

No one was there,
Was it her dream or just a nightmare?
Like every songs no matter how melodious it is
This also has to end at some instance.....
But she still thinks the song will again play
Intentionally or by chance.......

- Kumari Jyotsna

<u>Quest of white</u>

He always use to say
You look good in white.
But she never came to know,
Which white he meant??
Was it the white like the clouds?
Pure, light n above the business of the world.
Or it was like that of jasmine,
Whose innate nature was to make it's encircle
Fragrant.
May be it was the whiteness of that lotus in the pond,
Which shines with serenity despite being encircled
With weeds and mud.
Perhaps it was the white the color of her face when
The thought of even losing him came to her mind,
Like there is no blood flowing towards those checks
In any kind.
May be he meant the whiteness of the moonlight,
Filled with peace, clarity and mellow and wan.
Was it that white which everybody get wrapped in,
And get out of the trap of this world.
He always use to say

You look good in white,
But she never came to know,
She never knew which white it was.

- Kumari Jyotsna

Atharva Bhoyarkar

IG: _thewordaddictbong_

Basically from Nagpur, the city of oranges is a boy named Atharva Bhoyarkar. He loves to portray his emotions and thoughts on the paper in the form of poems. He is a protest poet (the person who address to real socio-political issues and express objection against them). He is fond of reading books. He is a passionate photographer. His nature of living he loves to help others and thinking for them before he thinks of himself makes him happy. He is a dog lover.

<u>Poetry</u>

When my eyes are locked with his
My lips are longing for his kiss
I feel a love I've never known
Yet my heart feels so alone
When our bodies are intertwined
And his hand is locked in mine
We're laying there cheek to cheek
Listening to our souls speak
We share our dreams, we share our fears
We're not afraid to shed our tears
We can cry and we can laugh
But we're burdened by our pasts
Jealousy begins to swell
Why can't happiness just prevail
Laughter always turns to anger
Our love is once again in danger
Good times don't ever seem to last
We can blame that on our past
Life has made us who we are
We never seem to get too far,
My soul will never really know
How to ever let you go
This love we have was unexpected
My heart is left unprotected,
I feel our paths were meant to cross
Before you, my soul was lost
Life's journey's leading me to you
I need us both to see this through,
I want a love that others envy
And a heart that isn't empty
I want you to cause my biggest smiles
Ones that can be seen for miles,

How can our story ever start
If we won't open up our hearts
I never want our love to end
You're my lover and my best friend,
I'm willing to work to make this last
Leaving our pasts in the past
Love builds from trust, honesty, and respect
I'll give it to you and it's what I'll expect,
So don't give up on what we have
Let's build it up and make it last
It'll be worth it, I promise you this
Our love is one that we would miss
My heart and soul are lost without you
Let's let love's destiny see us through
You're my soulmate, you were made for me
You're my heart's final destiny.

-Atharva Bhoyarkar

<u>My love craves for your love</u>

isn'tit strange,
how crazy i can get.
It's been months that you left,
and my eyes are still wet.
Isn't it strange,
how a soul can crave.
Your feelings are resting in peace,
and mine are still searching for a grave.
Isn't it strange,
how a person can change?
I was a happy soul earlier,
and now on the puzzle of rearrange.
Isn't it strange,

how eyes can wait?
My love is in abundance,
and so is your hate.
Isn't it strange,
how bad things are?
You are my moon,
so close to me,yet so far.
Isn't it strange,
how every song can relate.
We are together in my dreams,
but what about this fate?
Isn't it strange,
how life can confess?
A broken soul is surviving every day,
And yet feeling breathless.
Isn't it strange,
how a heart is in war?
It carries its own love,
and still craves for your.

-Atharva Bhoyarkar

<u>Shivangi Gupta</u>

IG: rainbow_p_e_a_r_l_s

Bio: "There are many times, you can't express your feelings, I got too express this by my pen" .Shivangi gupta currently in Ranchi, jharkhand. She is passionate about her writing. Till now she had been part of three Anthologies, she loves to be in Imaginative world of hers...she is fond of reading books.....

<u>The Princess in the crystal cell</u>

The sparkles and the bubbles

Slapping the trouble

All over the crystal cell

Can't invade the song in it

Art Thou wrapped in silk

The brown eye with curls

Thou no more a happy soul

Wherein she dwells in a crystal cell

Too strong, too thick

Neither let her disappear

Within the shadow of light

Nor let her escape

From the fracture of light.

She sense a smile

But their a grief inside

Round and Round

In the carousel how it goes

O men, O men

She seems alone

Art Thou forfeit, not a boon

Aura full of life, infusing the love outside

Within the amiss fate

That she hate

Someone will walk towards the crystal cell

From the undisclosed fog and snow

Thy break the spell

And her woefull tale

O Prince, O Prince

You are there for me

Thou Happiness shall overtake

As remorse harass bends

Art Thou longing ends

In the blaze of light

He grabs her hand

As walking out the crystal cell

She ain't not wink

As the bright eyes

We're aiming for it

Beauty get enrolled

As the steps walking towards the chariot

And the clouds and stars

Are the evidence of love in it.

-Shivangi Gupta

<u>I fall for him again</u>

The ocean was calm

Hiding the warmness in night

We stood their declining

All the commotion and

Scattered it all around the sand.

With two chairs and one benches

And a flower in middle

He pulled it for me

And gave a flower to me

And their I fall for him again

The Whispers of two soul

Holding the hand

Glaring beauty of ocean

In front of flames

Sparkling all around with

Smoky rays

Letting remember memos

In their ways

Where the fire seems seen

In his eyes

As pain lost in bonfire,

And he tuned the guitar

Their a born a new star in front of me

And their I fall for him again....

- Shivangi Gupta

CO-AUTHORS

<u>Who Will Love Me The Way You Love?</u>

I Come In Your Heart,
Whenever You Take A Deep Breath.
Through The Lanes of Your Heart,
I Pass By Every day.
I Move Like The Force Of Wind,
Where You Accompany Me In The Flow Like The Granules Of Sand.
Who Will Love Me The Way You Love??
The Journey Of Your Search For Your Beloved Stops At Me.
You Secretly Read What My Heart Says,
Because You Read My Eyes When I Am Unaware Of It.
By Meeting Me You Forget Your Dreams.
You Find Your Happiness And Smile In Me.
When You Put Your Hands In Mine,
You Feel Like Flying In That Moment.
Who Will Love Me The Way You Love?

©saswatbarry19

-Saswat Baral

<u>The Innocence of Love</u>

Whenever I See You Smiling, It Makes My Day.

Your

Gave Light to My Nights.

Your Grace Dominated Over My Male Ego and Made Me Bow to You.

I Will Walk With You So Close As Your Shadow Is To You.

I Will Pen This Lovely Moments Filled with Lovelorn Feelings asa Poem.

Oh My Girl!! Oh My Honey!! Oh My Beautiful Soul!!

You Are My Kurunji Flower, Where I Make Sure That I Will Never Make You Feel Blue.

©saswatbarry1

-Saswat Baral

<u>Grey Skie</u>

There's a lingering taste of water.
After a heavy down pour,
on everything.
The trees, the earth, the wind, on you.
You look up and ask, 'Do grey skies ever turn to blue?'
There's mud on your shoes.
Clothes drenched.
It's hard to make out whether the water droplets on your face are that of the rain
or from your eyes.
You smile. Looking at the vast stretch.
Do the grey ever turn to blue?
You ask again.
Or do they remain the same?
Blocking the sun forever.
Making every day mundane.
Every minute of your life unbearable, brainsick, unremarkable.
Your hands up towards the sky trying to clear the sky of the grey.
Your fragile fingers exposed.
There's bruise marks on your palms from holding on to the hurt for too long.
The sky remains the same.
Shame.
Ah, it starts to rain again.
The cloud bursts heavier this time.
Yet, you stand your ground.
Do grey skies ever turn to blue?
The water washes you not only from the outside.
It washes the soil and takes it somewhere far away.
Your skin visible through the rain soaked cloth.
Your eyes closed not meant to open until the heaven's door closes and the sky
changes colour.
Salvation comes in different forms.
Your grey skies have turned to blue.
However, patches remain just like the smile on your face.
You were never meant to remain the same.

-Arpan Vineet lakra

<u>Hey Mommy.</u>

Mommy here I am.
This world scares me no more.
Shadows of the past haunt me no more.
Mother, have I forgotten you?
Do you feel lonely without me there by your side?
My soul, my soul is guilty of not caring much when I should have.
Hiding beneath the leaves of busyness.
Conundrum of life, that's the way the world works I tell myself.
I lie, I lie.
I am guilty of not caring much when I should have.
When should I care, what must I do?
Care now. Call you up now.
Hey Mommy.
Hey.
How are you?
I am good, am at work.
Okay, do you have time?
Yes, say.
am doing good Mommy, I am healthy, I am holding my ground, I am growing.
Each day, everyday.
That's good. I am proud of you. I will see you soon. Gotta go back to work. Bye.
Bye Mummy.
The phone still on my ear. No one can hear but me.
I am so proud of you too. You go on, without stopping. Looking after me. I miss you and I love you. Don't you worry? I am taking care of myself and I have people who are around me. I am, I am learning. Growing each day, everyday. I am here. Scared no more. I am here. To take care.

-Arpan Vineet Lakra

<u>Let it go</u>

Human lives began at the dawn of the great era when dinosaurs vanished and the storm cleared of silence and darkness.

Before this era began we humans were hopeless and didn't used to talk much, now in the present we talk pretty well in our own respective ways but still we have to go a far way into learning our power of speech.

Human's developed a power through what they use to communicate but alas that also was false power because we weren't aware that this power does harm and good at the same time.

Lying became the new trend and at the same time telling the truth required more proof than telling a lie. A man can lie to your face and you would believe him and a person will bring a number of proofs to tell you the truth and still you would doubt him.

It's said in ancient texts that there was a time when we humans didn't use our vocal power we were still harnessing that power and in the meantime we all used to communicate just with hand signs and telepathy.

I think that would have a cool form of communication as you could always listen to the thoughts of everyone around you. Wish I could also do that, in today's time (21st century).

It's just a myth and I don't have any proof to justify my statement. Truth is a valuable asset if you use it well, it can save life's and make you a hero, for whatever it's worth, but sometimes telling the truth requires immense amount of strength. "Telling truth requires strength?"

Don't be shocked you must have experienced this at least once in your life that truth can be hard to tell and lying is as easy as winking an eye. This is so because we the human race were gifted with so many gifts that it confuses us among ourselves that what should we do, we can speak, we can walk, we can build, but the best thing we can think.

Thinking is progressive but it's a curse too, coz we think selfishly only for ourselves and don't value anyone else's opinion. So when we have a choice to tell the truth for something that we know is right we tell the truth, but when we have a choice to hide the truth or manipulate it we choose the latter, we do so to save ourselves from any harm or getting our good name spoiled.

I just want to say that don't be afraid to raise your voice to tell the truth and help someone out, or help yourself and get trapped in a loop of guilt for the rest your life, coz 'we do what has been done to us' this is vicious cycle that does more harm than good, 'do good and good will be done to you' is a nice principle to live your life by.

Finally I just want to say that you can do whatever you want to but just consider this before telling a lie or being selfish that if we lie to someone then they lying to us shouldn't make a difference coz we also did the same to them, we cheat somebody, somebody cheats us, and the cycle continues so it shouldn't matter right? But we still get mad at these petty reasons.

This is the modern age my friend's here if you do bad be ready to face even worse then what you did, here everyone just need one messily little reason to return you the favour you did them with interest and watch you while you suffer then stuff that same feeling of pain and agony in your face and tell you that you were the one that was wrong.

It's still not too late we can still change for the better even a handful of people can start a reason to make people understand this reason of hatred and this cycle of revenge. All we need to do is a simple task that is take all that hate and burn it inside us so that it doesn't spill out in the world coz when we leave this planet we take everything with us, all that hate will go with you but if you burn it now you can hopefully take some smiles with you when you leave.

A thought to make you think, 'Does all that hate I have inside me really deserve to be there or can I just let it go…

-Tarun Jeevnani

<u>You</u>

In your eyes I see,

Inside of it flawless and natural beauty.

Inside of you is a soul so clear,

A pure and loving heart without fear.

In your voice I can hear,

A lovely woman so dear.

In your lips so comely,

It is you, I want so badly.

In your smile so bright,

Your happiness to me it enlights.

In your hair so smooth,

And your sweetness like a fruit.

In you there is somebody I found,

My heartbeats in perfect harmony and sound.

Even if in love there is a lot of pain,

In your love I will always remain.!!!

-Saarthak Lakhani

<u>Dream</u>

I dreamt of you last night
Your soft lips, Against mine
The warmth of your body
Close to my frozen soul
Your loyalty and love
Unchanged; in this cruel world
GOOD MORNING, MY LOVE!
You said to me while pulling me closer
if this is a dream and I am drunk
I do not want to be sober..!
I crave you whole,
Not simply for skin
That rests on your bones,
But for the mind
Behind your eyes,
The heart that loves
Inside your ribs
And the fire that
Burns within your soul..!

-Saarthak Lakhani

<u>Colors would it be green or blue today?</u>

May be white my favorite dark a dark voice in the back of my mind offered no color at all as an alternative. I smoothered that voice the days of no color were simply too hard to born I needed color today.

A rainbow is a huge canvas of beautiful colours. Poems too are a mirror or the emotions having various shades and colors
Each poem represent a unique feeling life has gifted me
I try not to be verbose but with the help of poetry I bright light to my unspoke words and feelings. As poetry is a language understood only by pen I truly believe this is just a droplet of water fallen in to the vast sea of my emotions and words as there is so much more that needs to be explore by the wish and grace of god.

-Mohit Birla

<u>Poetry</u>

A life in colour
the pink of your cheeks
when the cold wind bites
theintricacy of your iris
against the blank of white
the darkness of sorrow. The
Green eye of the monster
When consumes your today and
Tomorrow the silver of wisdom
the green shoots that thrive
Embrace every colour
for they prove we are alive.

-Mohit Birla

<u>Poetry</u>

I am fall in love with you
Ever since I meet you
I 've had these feeling deep inside
Mainly ,when you hold me and look into my eyes I lose in you
You changed my world with blink of your eyes .
You just don't know what you have done for me.
You really are angle of my life that sent from above, Take care of me and
shower with love.

When I am with you time passes immediately,
I can forgot the world, when I am with you
When I had first meet you , I did not think that you would be mine.

Even today, sometimes it's seem that this is not a dream.
I want to settle in your heart for life time in whatever situation, Because I
Seem a God in You…

-Prince Thakur

The birth of fairy tale

Once upon a time there in dense valley of mind lived a girl called imagination. Imagination was a notorious girl she use to play around with small kids called memories in mind valley. She was so charming that she became the attention of mind valley, each and every little memory loved imagination. She gradually grew up and matured.

One day in the valley came threat called challenge. Challenge was known to be tough once challenge captured knowledge and depressed mind valley. Our memory kids was so much in threat of challenge that it stopped coming out to play. The challenge became more powerful. There was no hope that can save the imagination and her friends. So imagination packed her bags and decided to leave the town and never come back again.

While leaving valley in night imagination met a guy called silence. Imagination asked silence for help. Silence smiled and said yes. Then silence and imagination teamed up and went to fight challenge.

But they required a bigger fellow to defeat him. Silence and imagination designed a opponent but they failed several times. Imagination lost hope but silence was happy. Silence now had long duration of failures called Discovery. Silence knew what went wrong and corrected it.

Early morning mind valley saw challenge defeated. Everybody was shocked including memory how challenge was killed in mind valley. Silence then replied for the first time.

Your silence becomes father when intelligence is born out of womb of imagination the duration is often called discovery this is enough to kill any challenge of mind valley.

Dr Tilak Dixit

<u>Quotes</u>

To see yourself unbent

Go to that Extent

Have an Argument or

Take a Consent

But just reinvent the Present

Dr. Tilak Dixit

Let your anger live

Inside you

No one can care better

Besides you.

Dr. Tilak Dixit

<u>Poetry</u>

In the silhouette,

I found her soul,

Pure yet cold,

Her innocence softened my heart,

In the most beautiful way.

She murmured

Can we be friends?

To her perplexity,

I replied why not.

That day I realize,

What merriness is...

- Nikku Chān

<u>Poetry</u>

You owe me, the time

You called my name for the first time.

That day sun shined,

As it was mine.

Flowers bloomed,

In a gloomy room.

My heart beat skipped,

Every bit.

You owe me, every single time,

Your hugs keeps me fine.

But then,

Everything changed,

And it was strange,

Maybe the destiny,

Was taking its way,

Through a nasty gateway.

Still bearing the pain,

And wearing your name.

-Nikku Chān

<u>When I fell in love</u>

When I fell in love

The stars fell with me

My heart refused to beat

As his heartbeat was rhythm enough

When I fell in love

The skies sighed with me

The sun rays kissed me

As his breath was muse enough

When I fell in love

The city lights flickered

The streets were lonely

As his existence was company enough

When I fell in love

You fell with me

Stars in our eyes

Clouds on your fingertips

Lights in our hearts

The world was a symphony

As our love was music enough...

-Nikita Malik

<u>Billion undone worlds</u>

Sometimes I have an urge

To destroy the sunshine

Existential crises

Amongst the thousand embedded lies

Sometimes I have a wish

To split open the sky

Head splitter

Is what they call every undone deed when it dies

Sometimes I have a dream

To mark down the ocean

Into a billion undone worlds

We

Will only survive the death of time

It's only us

In this God-forsaken world

Who does not deserve to die…?

-Nikita Malik

<u>Quiet Place</u>

Where it's just my ink and I

Where it's just I and my muse

Where it's just i and myself

Quiet place where I can brood in peace

Where my blood turns into ink

Where my ink flows without hindrance

Where I can pen down my feelings

A quiet place where I can be in perfect solitude

I need to be in a quiet place to think

Even though I might be be a noisy person

A quiet place is where I need to be to pour my mind out onto paper

A quiet place where my pen can assume it's duties

A quiet place where I choose to be my kingdom

My quiet place where I rule all the demons in me

My quiet place where I can be who I always dream to be.

Somewhere in the outskirts of the town.

-Kshitij Anand

<u>Breaking Stereotype — from an engineering girl</u>

Being a woman in a man's world isn't simple. Not easy in the slightest degree."

They said she scored well because The Professor changed into partial for her.
She completed all her assignments, studied day and night time to satisfy her
figure's desires and all her classmates stated was "she is teacher's puppy "She
became known as an attention seeker just because she wore her preferred
lipstick to the classroom
Why can't she be intelligent if she looks beautiful

Why she can't be good at sports if she is smart
And the list of those why simply goes on increasing. Being a woman in a man's world isn't always easy. She constantly has to work a bit harder, a little greater, just to prove herself to be as worthy as her male counterpart. The mentality that only a boy can do engineering has dominated the engineering field for over the years
When she was younger, she was requested to stay far from cars, motorcycles and even more they are stored faraway from gas cylinders saying "you are a girl, gentle and smooth, don't play with these, you would possibly get harm" I mean truly dude!! Who will bear her duty when she grows up, you??

Any place she go she get the consideration of practically every one of the men around me! She can't go anyplace alone without inclination ungainly and awkward unfailingly!! In any case, in USA the things are somewhat better. Work investment of ladies is high here thus people barely feel alone The subsequent thing is she can't be pleasant to anybody regardless of whether she need to! Individuals misconstrue. She need to show off mentality to fend off them (despite the fact that I don't care for it). Everybody is pleasant to you. You don't have the foggiest idea who is extremely agreeable and who is being a tease.

Be it proving your value ,or making a spot on the basis of your ability in a male-dominated world it takes every ounce of patience and hard work ,simply to make your voice loud and clear , just to let people hear the voice of your capabilities,, but they're "THE ladies", The most powerful being that may ever be created(Sorry for being a touch partial over here!), being capable of managing any scenario with outstanding power as well as absolute grace. The way in which we think about ourselves has the whole lot to do with how way we see ourselves being correctly recognized
"For women, it can feel like everything we do comes with a price
Possibly this is on the grounds that such huge numbers of us comprehend what it resembles to die of life inside our very own bodies or perhaps this is on the grounds that such huge numbers of need to pay a high cost to try and progress toward becoming moms, yet in any case, it can feel hard to be a lady and a mother who feels like she is continually making exchange offs just to endure the day

-Kshitij Anand

<u>Family violence</u>

Family violence is also known by other names like DOMESTIC VIOLENCE, INTIMATE PARTNER VIOLENCE, DATING VIOLENCE, SPOUSAL ABUSE, and DOMESTIC ABUSE. This takes place in many forms and can be seen in many families, but no one is ready to talk about it openly just because people find that domestic violence is common and it occurs in every form of family. We can see it be it is married or unmarried couples. Domestic Violence causes far more pain than the visible marks of bruises and scars. It is devastating to be abused by someone that you love and think loves you in return. With the fear of not letting it known to society, no one could share because the so-called "SOCIETY" would judge them. But what happens if one person tries to share about it?? There are many families where it still takes place and it does affect the entire family even if the violence is between the two people. They don't see in anger that what are their children learning or what impact will be on them, after seeing this. Let's say there's a child whose name is "AARIEL", at her place she used to see domestic violence, at one phase of her life she used to see it on her daily basics. When it happened for the first time she thought that it may not go to that much seriousness, but no it did went to the extreme level. She thought that it would be between the parents but no!! She was wrong. One fine day when she came back home after her classes she was tired and was just resting and was reading the news on her phone and her siblings were playing games on their phone. Then all of a sudden her father entered the room where all they were and snacked Aariel's phone saying "that you are not studying". Hearing this she was confused because she just came home from her classes and when her father snacked her phone Aariel's phone got broken about which she got angry because she got that phone from her first salary when she used to work. In anger she was going to the other room and then her father just grabbed her hair and pulled her back. When all this happened no one said anything to the father not even her mother and neither her siblings. And all day long after this incident she was broken down that how could her father do this to her and wondered why didn't no one from the family stopped her father even after seeing it. All-day she was thinking about it she got a very severe headache for which she was hospitalized and was on an overdose of medicine because she wasn't able to sleep properly after that incident. Even for sleeping, she was taking pills. When she was discharged from the hospital her father just said to her, "DON'T THINK TOO MUCH". And she was blank at that moment that what should she not think, about that just few hours earlier her father had grabbed her hair or she should not think about that no one from the family objected her father on his such action or she should not think about all the mental and psychological trauma that she's going through. Even though she's had been discharged from the hospital but her mental condition is not well because of her father and neither she is not able to sleep without having the medicines. She got her hair cut because she doesn't want any person like her father to grab her hair for abusing her because ABUSE is NOT Love. Abuse is about control and were a house where a woman is unsafe is not a home.

Deepti lakra

<u>Journey of Love</u>

Everything happens for a reason
I believe this statement to be true;
That's why you were sent to me and I was sent to you...
As a desert creature longs for water,
My thirst for you can never be slaked…
My days are filled with craving,
My nights are full of dreams,
I'm always thinking of you
I'm in a glaze, it seems..
Yes we fight,
And I've lied
But our heart has been permanently touched…
Once there was a deep dark hole nobody could touch,
Until you came and filled it with all your love…
I want to be with you the rest of my life,
Until the day I say good-bye..!!

-Sneh Antil

<u>A wish for Peace</u>

When span of sorrow
Come each day,
I always feel blue,
And sigh away...
Everyone that was within its Path,
Had pleated their hands to Prey.
Asking to make it their Anthem
So peace could have its own Day.
Always a war, needs fighting
Always a life, suffering…
Oh! How I wish,
I wish for Peace…
A time of love…

A time of leisure;
Oh! How I wish,
I wish for Peace...
As trees and flowers sway
And the wind blows away
It brings in a new blink of hope
That return peace can still recoil…
It showed everyone a new beginning,
That each and Every one could accept.
A harmony of spirit,
And comfort of courtesies…
Security for our beloveds and their beloveds,
With none of them looking back
"Giving Peace a Chance" being kept...!!
We, cherubs and living souls,
Believers and Non-believers,
Look heavenward and speak the word aloud
PEACE.....
We look at each other than into ourselves,
And say without apologue or shyness
Peace my Brother/Sister;
Peace my Parents;
Peace my Soul;
Peace my WORLD...

-Sneh Antil

<u>Sky Full of Energies!!!</u>

What's the very first thing that strikes your mind, when your eyes meet the sky?? . It's 12:25am and I am standing in my terrace, everything around me is drenching in water, taking a look first to the right and then to the left, all I can see is the night consuming the surroundings slowly, bit-by-bit, filling it with a weirdly satisfying silence. My eyes adjusting with the darkness of night as it rain, i turn the volume low, watching the clouds pass by and now a part of black sky is trying to peep down. Have you taken a look at the sky in the dark, the peace it reflects, has the power to heal. The power to heal each and every brave warrior's heart which has been injured in the battle, fought in the name of LOVE. We as entities are living in a magical world, where our vibes speak louder as compared to us, energies are released from the human body in the form of LOVE, HAPPINESS, ANGER, SORROW, GUILT, HATRED, JEALOUSY & JOY, and these sentiments are subdivided into unsaid words. SOME EXPRESSED AND SOME SUPPRESSED. Night sky plays a very important role in this scenario!!

How?

According to psychology, a hide tide of emotions thwacks a human mind and heart, during the phase of late nights and early mornings. When we as humans releases any sort of energies regarding any subject, the universe makes sure that the energies reaches its destination to skelps that entity.

Example: 1). In the case of Love, if your loved ones are far away and it has been ages you haven't met them, a wave of mixed feelings are released. At the very same time they are missing you, suddenly out of blue you get a call from them, and you jump joyfully saying "you'll live for a 100 years, was just thinking about you and you happened to call".

Example: 2). In case of Anger, when you just have an argument with your siblings over something and you decide not talking to each other, but because of some or the order reason you end up doing the same task, the gesture of anger given, even when not spoken, are again energies.

Example: 3). In the case of Happiness, when you look at your plant or pet (if you are a nature or animal person) the gush of joy that comes from within you reaches them and they too get happy. In plants they respond to you by growing well. In pets they jump in happiness around their owners. This game of energies, is not only played in humans but also in animals, plants actually every living being no matter even if it's the smallest insect. In other words, "ENERGY EXCHANGE", is a process in which two or more entities are involved. If the entity A is throwing a black ball (negative energies) to entity B, even if he is not thinking about any negative thing at the current moment, after coming in contact with this ball, B will also start thinking negative and the black ball will return back to A. Same goes for white ball (positive energies). Also known as TELEPATHY (the supposed communication of thoughts/ideas by means other than the known sense). Most of the black ball and white balls are exchanged in the night time and every time SKY witnesses it. No energies get cross connected like our telephone lines, because they have supernatural power. Be careful!! With what you thinking about other entities, the universe is very rapid in transmitting the energies, somewhere someone is thinking the same about you.

Bushra Sheikh
(Saeraa.S)

<u>Poetry</u>

She wanted to fly HIGH;
He accompanied her to see the SKY.
She is a rising GLORY;
and behind her He is her prompt STORY.
He kissed her as if he don't want to taste anything AFTER;
She kissed him as if she never tasted anything RATHER.
Nothing was more adorable than her hair FLICKS;
How could he resist himself to fall for her chubby CHEEKS.
But... But...
Stopped by the society, accused by the SPECIES;
to stay together till the last breadth was their DISEASE.
Past & Future; they didn't CARE;
for them to stay together; this was the DARE.
In the world full of DISPARAGE;
Communal harmony; they delivered the MESSAGE.
People doubted like poison CLOUD;
I just Love you they both shouted LOUD.
In the peanut crumbling CROWD;
yes, we accept each other as we are!
They spoke it all LOUD.
They spoke it all LOUD!

Vaidehi kathote

<u>An echo from the past!</u>

To the end, till I DIE;

Only you will owe me, I can TRY!♡

Hand in hand walking along the SEASHORE;

The sea too witnessed our love to the CORE! ♡

Separated by MILES;

United by SMILES! ♡

In the world prioritizing Physical INTIMACY;

I loved the way we maintained our SECRECY! ♡

It was a happy place, though I won't be able to VISIT;

No matter how hard I try, THAT phase from my Heart don't have anexit!

Intentional or Destiny, it doesn't MATTER;

As the time passes, my feelings would not SHATTER! ♡

Prose or Poetry WHATEVER;

You inspired me for both FOREVER! ♡

Arguments and Harsh words didn't work HERE;

Jingles all the way were EVERYWHERE!♡

Always ready to Dine with YOU;

Because I know that I will be Fine with YOU! ♡

Echo from the PAST!

-Vaidehi kathote

<u>Thoughts the little mess</u>

Thoughts keep knocking
Aloha!! are you there??
Peeping through the window
Bonjour!! are you there??
Hidden underneath the rug
Ola!! are you there??

Woah..
Easy easy
Steady a bit
Halt now!!
Worry imminent!!
In deep exasperation;
I take a stance and just decide to ask:

Thoughts why are you not in a check??
You just keep racing through, knocking off the vase, the conscience is indeed
worried
And the worry has put wrinkles on it's face
But NO...You were busy eating that word pastry.

Thoughts just glared me back with the utmost pleading eyes, and then
and then..??
Then??
You ask me what happened. Yes do read along. What little fella has done?
Back to the conversations with the thoughts.

The thoughts just stood there, yes it looked absolutely innocent. Something
which may absolutely melt your heart.

I ask thoughts back,

You ask why I know??
I ask you back,
Why are those letters sticking on to your face??

Why the mind's kitchen a mess??
Why the tumbling and toppling over the utensils??
Why the unrest?
Is it all a jest??

Being raw right from the start
bruising that very corner
something which is called heart;
'thought' being funny
and the candid best
keeps on circling the mind
not even worried for a rest
the kid is going out of hand; I proclaim

A moment of silence.
And then it starts again;
Aloha!! are you there??
Bonjour!! are you there??
Ola!! are you there??
A funny encounter with 'thought', the kid protagonist in the story
My friend from an imaginary world.

- Shalini Toppo

<u>Dear Dreams</u>

Beyond the galaxies

The sleepless deep darkness

You make meRavel through

Oh dear dream, you are mine

Every now and then

You manifest me to myself

Force me to extract the best in me

Your concern cares too much indeed

You drag me out of myself

You dip me throughout

Yourself and you in my self

Dear dream, my own self

Seldom have I got out of you

Love for me yours is unmeasurable

This nameless and tagless relation exists

Dear dream, I am all yours

Brighter than the Sun

Together you and I shine

You never concede my slumber

You make me ameliorate, more and more

Unveiling my potential

You've ignited a flame

Lighted it will be till I breathe

Until you and I meet and greet

So passionate I am to see you

For sure, I will embrace you!!

-Aditi Nayak

<u>My beloved</u>

Hiding your secret tears

You affectionately bless me

Showing your sweetest smile

You inspirit every bit of me

Termless and timeless is your care

So heartily innocent you deeply are

Not ever I saw your failure

Certainly you were sent from the stars

Giving me plenteous courage

Enabling to conquer every trouble

Pretty lucky I am

Oh beloved grandmother, all my love is yours

Listen O Almighty!

You may bounce my wishes back

It's your choice but do

Consider the prayers of my beloved…

-Aditi Nayak

"कामयाबी"

तेरी जरूरतों से आगे बढ़

कुछ हालातों से फासला रख

शिकायतों से भरीपडी हे जेबें यहाँ

बस्सतू तेरा अभिमान ज़िंदा रख

तू आसमान से उंचा बन

तानें समाने की क्षमता रख

कभी तो खत्म होगा इंतजार कामयाबी का

बस्सतू तेरी कोशिशे जारी रख

-Kartik Powar

"मुसाफिरवो"

मुझें इक घर बनाकर ठेहेरना था
वो मुसाफिर थी, बहोत दूर जाना चाहती थी

-Kartik Powar

"झप्पी"

अचानक आयी ठंड तुम्हारी याद साथ लाई
बंद आँखों के सामने पहली झप्पी दिखा गई

-Kartik Powar

<u>Poetry</u>

वह सब लौट आएंगे

जिसने छोड़ दिया था,

बुरे वक्त में तेरा साथ वह

मिट्टी से भी सोना निकाल लाएंगे,

तुम एक बार कामयाब तो होजाओ,

वह सब लौट आएंगे

यह छोटी सोचवाले तुम्हें रोज

नोच नोचकर खाजाएंगे,

तुम्हारे इस लड़ाई कामजाक भी उड़ाएंगे,

तुम एक बार कामयाब तो होजाओ,

वह सब लौट आएंगे

वक्त की कशमकश में खो ना जाना,

हर दिन नए मौके आएंगे आसमान में तुम्हारे नाम की भी तारे टीम

टीमाएगे,

तुम एक बार कामयाब तो होजाओ,

वह सब लौट आएंगे

यकीन रख पर खुद पर

अंधेरे में भी तीर चलाएंगे,

अगर चुक गया अंदाजा

तो एक नया तीर बनाएंगे,

सबर कर...

काबिल बन जाएंगे

पैसा इज्जत दौलत वह सब लाएंगे,

वह खुद क्या खुदके बापको भी लाएंगे,

तुम एक बार कामयाब तो हो जाओ,

वह सब लौट आएंगे

-Mr Sandesh Pathaihe

Poetry

प्यार चाहिए

ना वफा का खुला आसमान चाहिए,

ना आंसुओं की बारिश की बूंदों में लिपटी तनहाई चाहिए,

जिंदगी जीने के लिए

प्यार चाहिए

ना करें मुझे अनदेखा अनजान समझकर ऐसा इंसान चाहिए,

जिसका दिल टूटा हो चलेगा पर उसे दिल जोड़ते आना चाहिए,

जिंदगी जीने के लिए

प्यार चाहिए

हो जाए गलती उसे तो समझा दूंगा, पर हो मेरी गलती तो मुझे समझने

वाला चाहिए,

खामोशी नहीं सही,

पर आंखों को पढ़ने वाला यार चाहिए

जिंदगी जीने के लिए

प्यार चाहिए

-Mr Sandesh Pataihe

Quotes

Reciting the rhythm

Of your heart beat

While Painting the

Colours on your soul

Have become my

Most favourite pass-time.

-Shilpa Krishna

<u>Poetry</u>

Years have gone by,

But your kiss has rooted

So deep to be forgotten.

It gave boundless

Hope of tomorrow and

So much more than that.

You may not realize

For some reason how

You warm my heart all day

Shall we create some

Memories all over again?

Will you be mine?

-Shilpa Krishna

<u>Silent Love</u>

It was not love at first sight

It was something more than attraction

Something connected their hearts as one

They fell unwillingly for the other

They were imperfectly perfect for each

Imperfections made them to fall in love

They started to care unknowingly

As if some soulful connection was there

Unconfessed feelings were waiting

Messed up thoughts created a new hope

Someone started to rule independent heart

As if destiny had already planned the best part

The moment they realised was itself perfect

Still they waited for the right time to come

To express what they actually feel

They tried their luck by not saying a single word.

-Jaspreet Kaur

<u>Love and seperation</u>

No more they are together

Still they care for each other

There are differences between them

But they never spoke ill of the other

They separated for some reasons

Still something connected their hearts

They learnt how to ignore the other

But their souls don't want to be apart

Perfectly matched they were for the other

Still some imperfection ruled their relation

One can't say they hated the other

It was about love they had in their relation

Situations might have resulted in separation

Still they have some unshared feelings to share

One more story ended in wait of realisation

It was all about the affection which was once there….

-Jaspreet Kaur

<u>बतादेना...</u>

कोइ हमारी तरह चाहे तो बता देना,

कोइ हमारी तरह सता ये तो बता देना,

अरे,

प्यार मोहोब्बत तो हर कोइ कर लेगा तुमसे,

कोइ हमारी तरह निभाए तो बता देना...

कोइ हमारी तरह रुह, जान एक कर प्यार करे तो बता देना,

अपनी जिंदगी अपने कम तुम्हारे नाम ज्यादा करे तो बता देना,

लोग तो आ जाया करेंगे तुम्हारे जिंदगी में अक्सर,

हमारी तरह कोइ सब्र कर बस आपके इंतजार में रहे तो बता देना...

तुम्हारी छोटी छोटी खुशी में दुनिया ढुंडे तो

बता देना,

तुम्हारी हर जिद्पुरी करने कि पुरे जीयो जान से कोशिश करे तो बता

देना,

दिखाने के लिये तो लोग अक्सर ही प्यार जताया करते हैं,

कोई आप पे अपना सब कुछ नौछावर करदे तो बता देना...

युंही नहीं मिलते हैं लोग खुले रासतों में आजकल,

और मिल भी गयें तो मंजिल तक साथ चलनें किता कद भी नहिं रखते,

अपने अच्छे वक्त में तो हर कोई हाथ थाम लेगा तुम्हारा,

बुरे वक्त में कोई हमारी तरह हौसला दिखाये तो बता देना...

-विक्रांतमोहरीर

<u>Yeah I know</u>

Yeah I know, you thought it wasn't love

Coz' it happened just in couple of days

Yeah I know you never loved me

But who cares, coz I still do

Yeah I know you have another one in your life,

But who cares, coz it won't affect my emotions

Yeah I know you were only with me on your bad days

But who cares, coz I'm habitual to darkest life

Your measurements were based on time lapse and mine were true feelings..!!

You were just giving it a try and I was pouring my heart beats..!!

You were attracted towards me as my straight expressing nature impressed you,

And I was in love with your soul..!!

You were still taking a time and I declared it directly as never ending love..!!

Yeah I'm too sure about my feelings at this moment

It's been 4 and half months since we both uttered a word but still it isn't able to crack the magnitude of my affection towards you..!!

You truly deserve this and I don't deserve it but life is all about luck..!!

-Vikrant Mohrir

<u>मां</u>

तू मुझसे दूर न होना,
ना मैं तुझसे होऊंगा।
तेरी कॉल जो ना आई माँ
सच्ची बहुत मैं रोऊंगा।।
नन्हा हूँ मैं अभी भी तेरा,
ये बोझ कहाँ से धोऊंगा।
उठाये जो आवाज़ ना तेरी,
मैं अंत समय तक सोऊंगा।।
तेरी सूखी रोटी के आगे,
हर छप्पन भोग भुलाऊंगा।
सब काम करूंगा खुदसे मैं,
अब और ना तुझे सताऊंगा।।
गले भी लगूं गा मैं तुझसे,
तेरे पैर भी खूब दबाऊंगा।
एक बार मुझे बस घर ले चल,
यहाँ लौट कभी ना आऊंगा।

-Nikhil Tiwari

दफना आया

उन कसमों को, वादों को

वहीं दफना आया हूँ......

वहीं जहाँ धीमी सी मुस्कान के साथ पलकें झुक गयी थीं

वहीं जहाँ छूते ही घबराकर तुमने कहा कोई देख न ले

वहीं जहाँ इंतज़ार ने बेकरार किया था।

उस इंतज़ार को, उसी प्यार को

वहीं दफना आया हूँ।

वहीं जहाँ डटके खड़ी थी तुम मेरे लिए कभी

वहीं जहाँ उससे पूछा क्या लगती है वो मेरी?

जहाँ साथ पकड़ने जाने पर भी तुम भागी नही....

उन यादों को, उन्हीं बातों को

वहीं दफना आया हूँ

वहीं जहाँ बाहर जाता देख आंखें नम कर ली थीं

वहीं जहाँ मिलते ही मुश्किलें खत्म कर ली थीं

वहीं जहाँ मेरा फ़र्ज़, तुम निभाने लगी थी

खुदको, तुमको

बस वहीं दफना नै आया हूँ मैं।

-Nikhil Tiwari

<u>Poetry</u>

ज़िंदगी और मौत मे, यूँ फसके रह जाती हू |

मौत मुझे चाहती है,

मैं ज़िंदगी को चाहती हू!

कुछ यूँ रिझाती है, मौत मुझे,

मेरे आसपास मंडराती है,

मैं जहाँ जहाँ भी जाती हू

ये मेरे पीछे पीछे आती है,

मैं अनदेखा क़र दु, तो बुरा इसे लग जाता है!

दो बता ज़िंदगी से करलू, तो इसका दिल घबराता है,

मैं एक कदम बढ़ाती हू, ये साथ साथ मेरे चलती है.

मैं ज़िंदगी का हाथ थामु, तो ये मुझसे लड़ती है!

रूठ भले ही जाए, पर पीछा मेरा ना छोड़ती है!

मैं ज़िंदगी के पिछे हू, ये मेरे पिछे रहती है!

लड़ खड़ा मैं जाऊँ, तो ये दोनो हाथ बढ़ाती है!

ज़िंदगी घबरा जाती है, और मौत दाँत दिखाती है!

कुछ यूँ रिश्ता हम तीनो का,

हमे बाँधी एक ही डोरी है।

मैं ज़िंदगी के बिना अधूरी हूँ,

और मौत मेरे बिना अधूरी है।

रोज़ शाम की चाय पर, हमती नो गप्पे लगाते है,

मैं ज़िंदगी को देखती हू

मौत मुझे घुरे जाती है!

फिर इन दोनो को देख, मैं मन ही मन मुस्काती हू!

मौत मुझे चाहती है, मैं ज़िंदगी को चाहती हू

Swati Bharadwaj

<u>Poetry</u>

मुश्किलों के पिंजरे में कैद हम हैं तो मगर,

हम वो पंछी हैं जो कैद में भी आज़ाद से है।

हम पिंजरे से ही झांकते है,

सपनो के पुल बांधते है।

सोचते हम कुछ नहीं,जो मन कहे वो मानते है।

पिंजरा थोड़ा सख्त है,

खुलने में लेगा वक़्त है

आसानी से बहार न निकलेंगे, हम तो ये भी जानते है।

निराशाओं का पहरेदार,

पिंजरे के बाहर खड़ा,

अँधेरे साथी हैं उसके, वह क्रूर अभिमानी है बड़ा।

पर हम भी साहसी है बड़े, हम इतने से थकते नहीं।

गब्बर और मोगेम्बो के फैन है,छोटे मोटे विलनो से डरते नहीं ।

हम आशाओं की लालटेन ले, रोज़ चाबी खोजते है।

हम अँधेरे का फ़ायदा उठा, चुपके से सुरंग भी खोदते है

भूख प्यास की चिंता नहीं, गम और आंसू साथ है।

इन्ही को खापी कर हम, बाँधे हुए अपनी श्वांस है।

तुफानो के आने पर भी हम घबराते बिलकुल नहीं,

उनको तोह मरू रिश्तेदार जैसे कोई जानते है।

आंधियो का क्या कहे उनकी भी बात और है,

आंधियो को भी तो हम अपना बड़ा भाई मानते है।

निकलेंगे बहार तो ज़रूर, पर अभी यहीं पर सही।

छोटे पिंजरे में भी हम मस्ती और आराम से है

क्योंकि,

हम वो पंछी हैं जो कैदमें भी आज़ाद से है।

-Swati Bharadwaj

<u>Poetry</u>

यह बहती हवाएँ...
अकसर कुछ महसूस करा जाती है,
इस इंतज़ार भरे लम्हों के बीच...
अकसर उनके आनेकी आस जगजाती है.
उनकी वह तसवीर...

जिसे आज भी हम संजोए रखते हैं,
भले ही लफ्ज़ों से बयाँ न हो ये इश्क...
इन जस्बातों की उन्हे खबर रहती है.

चाहे कितनी भी दूरी बनी रहे,
चाहे हम मिलेया ना मिले,
जुड़ गए जो दिल के रास्ते,
ये फासले भी बस बहाने लगने लगे.

Shazeen Sania

<u>Poetry</u>

तुम्हारे जाने से कुछ पल रुकी तो थी यह जिन्दगी,

पर अब ठीक मेरे हालात हैं...

इस धड़कन में आज भी,

जगे तुम्हारे लिए एहसास हैं...

चाह थी जो तुम्हारे साथ पूरी जिन्दगी चलने की

पर अब टूटने लगी हर आस है...

देखे थे हमने जो वह सपने,

पर अब टूटने लगे वो ख्वाब हैं...

तुम आना कभी हमारी गली,

के इस गली को भी तेरा इंतजार है...

तेरे जाने से रुकी तो थी यह जिन्दगी,

पर, फिर भी, ठीक मेरे हालात हैं...

- Shazeen Sania

<u>वो लड़की</u>

वो जो ये चेहरे पे हल्की मुस्कान लाती है,

वो जो यूँ ब्लैक ड्रेस में मिलने आती है।

बिना किसी मेकअप के ही,

यूँ कुछ ऐसा कर जाती है।

मैं खड़ा उसे यूँ ही ताकता रहता हूँ,

और वो कुछ आँखों में ही कह जाती है।।

वो लड़की जो सांवले रंग की हूर सी मुझको लगती है,

मेरी चाय के रंग के जैसे खूबसूरत जँचती है।

एक मिठास लेकर सीरत में अपनी,

वो लाखों सूरत को मात देती है।

वो लड़की सूट में ऐसे जँच दी है,

पंजाबी कुड़ी बन मेरी नज़रों को कैद करती है।

वो जो यूँ मुझे कनखियों से देखती है,

मेरे दिल को एक सुकून सी देती है।

उसकी जो ये चलने में कोई शरारत है,

उसके जो ये बोलने में कोई इबादत है।

वो मेरी है या नही , पता नहीं

पर जो वो मेरे लिए है , वो शायद और कोई और नही। .

-Shobhit Kumar

दुपट्टा

मेरी मुहब्बत की कशिश, वो बेतरती बढा गयी

खुदा दुपट्टा वो अपने कांधे से जब सरका गयी

मुश्किल कर जो दिया मैंने, इज़हारे मुहब्बत

मुस्कुरा कर, दुपट्टे का कोना, दांतो तले वो दबा गयी।

एक नज़र भरके देख लूं, उसे छत पे जाकर मैं

धूपमें, नंगे पाऊं आकर, वो दुपट्टा लहरा गयी

सम्भलता नही दुपट्टा उससे, दिल क्या संभालेगी वो

इतना ही कहना था, के दुपट्टे से मेरा गला दबा गयी

उनके इश्क़ के रुबरु हैनी लो फर शख्सियत अपनी

क़बूल हूँ मैं उसे, ये कहकर वो लाल दुपट्टा थमा गयी।

Nilofar Farooqui Tauseef

चूड़ी

इस दिल पे भी, वो क्या सितम ढाती है

उंगली छूने नही देती, चूड़ी वाले को हाथ थमा देती है

उसकी हर खनक की आवाज़ क्या कहिये

सोये हुए को भी नींद से जगा देती है।

सोलह श्रृंगार क्या खूब सजता है उन पे

पर ये कांच की चूड़ी, चार चांद लगा देती है

इंद्रधनुष के रंगों में वो बात कहां

जो मेरे महबूब की कलाई को सजा देती है

आज भी ये दिल, धड़कता है नीलोफर

जब प्यार से वो चूड़ी की खनक सुना देती है।

Nilofar Farooqui Tauseef

<u>एकखत</u>

एकखत आज मैंने, अपने प्यार के नाम लिखा है

लबों पे खामोशी, लफ़्ज़ों में पैग़ाम लिखा है।

तराशा है क़ुदरतने, जिस खूबरसूरती से उन्हें

उनकी ही अदाका, छोटा सा फरमान लिखा है

क़बूल जो हो जाये, उन्हें मेरी भी उल्फत

हसीन लफ़्ज़ों को जोड़कर, एक अरमान लिखा है।

आईने में नज़र आता है, सिर्फ उन काही एक चेहरा

क्या चीज़ हैं वो मेरे, वही एक पहचान लिखा है

शर्म से पिघलने लगी है, स्याही नीलोफर

कहना ज़रा उनसे, हमने किस्सा तमाम लिखा है।

Nilofar Farooqui Tauseef

<u>पहला प्यार</u>

याद कर मेरा दिल जो तुझपे निसार था,

हां वो जो दबा दबा सा प्यार था।

तेरे सोख कदमो की धूल थी,

तेरा दिल भी बेकरार था

ज़रा यादकर ओ मेरे हम सफ़र मेरा दिल जो तुझ पे निसार था,

हां वो मेरे पहले इश्क का पहला खुमार था।

वो घुटी घुटी अरमान ए दिल

मेरी आहें दर्द की साज थी।

ज़रा याद कर ओ मेरे हम नवा, मेरा दिल जो तुझपे निसार था।

हां वो जो डरा डरा सा प्यार था।

जिससे रो दिया था मेरा ज़रा ज़रा,

वो मेरी बेबसी का इजहार था

ज़रा याद कर ओ मेरे हम नफ़स मेरा दिल जो तुझपे निसार था,

हां वो तेरी झील सी आंखों का चढ़ा मुझपे खुमार था।

हां मेरा भी दिल बेकरार था,

तेरा भी दिल बेकरार था।

- Vivek_jr.

राही

चल तू निडर होके,

बेख़ौफ़ तू बेसबर होके,

रूकना नहीं, ठहरना नहीं,

तू चल बेखबर होके,

तू राही हैं तेरे सपनों का,

तू चल हौसला ए जिगर लेके,

वक़्त के कांटे चुभेंगे, रोकेंगे

पर तू चल दर्द ए बेफिकर होके,

रोकेंगी कुछ आवाजें, भटकाएगी भी,

पर तू चल रेखा ए किरण होके,

पर वाह ना कर मंजिल की, वो तो मिलनी ही है,

बस तू चल राही ए मदमस्त होके,

ये उड़ान हैं तेरे सपनों की, तेरे हौसलौ की,

बस तू चल, कर दृढ़निश्चय ले के।

-Vivek_jr.

<u>Poetry</u>

आज फिर देखा उसे यादों में मैंने,

उसकी इस नज़ाकत के भी क्या कहने,

सुनाए उसने मुझे कई गीत यार के,

पर निकले ना उसके मन से अल्फाज़ कभी प्यार के,

इक बार फिर याद आई उसकी आज शाम में,

दिखने लगी वो हर जगह, ईश्वर, अल्लाह और राम में,

सोचा था ना देखूंगा- ना सोचूंगा उसके बारे में कभी,

बस खयाल आया ही था ये, मेरे मन में तभी,

पता है!! मेरी हर बात पे वो हस दिया करती थी,

मुझे लगता था जैसे, वो मुझपर ही मरती थी,

ना कह पाया कभी उससे अपने दिल के जज़्बात,

जब भी हुई उसकी मुझसे मुलाकात,

हां एक बार कोशिश भी की थी मैंने,

मुझसे अच्छी मिल जाएगी कहकर फिर टाल दी वो बात।

उसकी मुस्कुराहट में एक अलग ही था जादू,

जब भी उसको देखता, हो जाता था ये दिल बेकाबू,

उसके बारे में और क्या कहूं मैं यारों,

सारी उम्र बीत जाएगी जो एक - एक करके उसकी तारीफें सुनादुं।

इक बार फिर उसने हस के देखा ख्वाबों की उन वादियों में,

अब तो दूल्हे-दुल्हन की जगह हम दोनों का चेहरा दिखता था हर शादियों में,

कितना अच्छा लगता, हर लम्हा जो बिताता तेरे साथ,

मेरे नाम की मेंहदी से जो सजता तेरा हाथ,

पर कोई बात नहीं, किस्मत है सबकी अपनी अपनी,

हो सकता है इस दिल में किसी और की तसवीर थी छपनी,

तू मज़े कर, मैं अब भी हूं साथ तेरे हर डगर,

याद जरूर करना जो मुश्किल आए कभी, दोस्त मानती है अगर,

बस ऐसा कहकर चल दिया ख़्वाबों की उस दुनिया से मैं अकेला,

तब से इंतज़ार है मुझ मजनू को के कब आयेगी मेरी लैला,

मुझे ना मिली वो, पर एक एहसास दे गई मीठा,

अब भी दिल में था उसके प्यार के जाम का छींटा,

इक बार फिर मेहका गई वो मेरे दिल के फूल को,

चल पड़ा फिर उसकी राहों में, और इक बार फिर भूल गया मै अपने उसूल को,

इक बार फिर भूल गया मै अपने उसूल को।।

-Mahendra Keshwani

<u>Poetry</u>

इक मै हो, इक तू हो और रात हो

चाय भी साथ हो तो क्या बात हो

रफ़ी के गानों का फ़साना हो

"पास बैठो" का कई बार आना हो

खुले आम प्यार जताना हो

पुछना ना हो, बताना हो

हामियों मे सिर्फ़ सर हिलाना हो

तेरे सर का मेरे सीने पे आना हो

तेरा लबों से मुस्कुराना हो

दिल की बात जुबां पे आना हो

आँखों से सारी बाते समझाना हो

तेरा रूठना हो, मेरा मनाना हो

सिर्फ़ एक दूसरे की बाहों मे खोजाना हो

मेरी ग़लतियों पे तेरा गले लगाना हो

तू दूर जाये तो मेरा झट से बुलाना हो

मेरे प्यार मे तेरा प्यार से इतराना हो

शो ऑफ ना कर, ऐसा मेरा सिखाना हो

कुछ ऐसी हमारी मुलाक़ात हो

कहीं भी ना जाने की बात हो

किस्से खुलते रहें कुछ ऐसे

जैसे बटर ही खैरात हो
और जब जाने का समय आए
सुकूं भी हो और मलाल हो
कि काश ये चाय कुछ देर बाद ठंडी होती
काश ये रात कुछ और लंबी होती।

-**Aman Rai**

<u>Poetry</u>

I've seen your flaws, your lapses and cross.

I don't ask you "why?"

I've seen how you lose patience on things.

How your mood suddenly swings.

I've seen all of your imperfections.

Regardless of all these weaknesses in you,

I still love you.

Love is never confined in a small area of beautiful things.

It also includes the acceptance of all the negativities, a person possess.

And with these, I offer you a love, which never questions.

A love in which you don't have to explain everything.

A love, in which you'll just feel comfortable, careless, and simply be safe about it.

A love that never judges, and never holds any grudge.

A love which is exclusive for you.

I can't promise to not make you cry, but I assure you, it's the least thing that I can possibly do.

I can't promise you to always make you feel good, but I assure you, you won't never feel unimportant or left out.

I do hope that you'll never fear in showing your real self with me. Because loving you at your worst, is the best thing that I can do to make you feel first and number one.

First in my heart.

First in my priorities.

And first in my life.

I loved you first, and I'll make sure this will be my last....

-Nemika Sharma

<u>Poetry</u>

I dream not in my dreams,

My poems are not poetic.

I say its pain when thy glee is what i write.

I admit its cliche, it's cryptic

For what i am, if not a mere piece of your stories?

Thou my scars make me, my emotions break me

Still i find peace in what they call strange.

Maybe a 90's rusted book, with violins tuning out of my life.

My destiny tells me,

One day, they'll repeat

She dreamnt not in her dreams,

Her poems were not poetic.

-Avni Arneja

<u>Roses</u>

I perceive myself as a beguiling rose

My past has been beautiful, my future's uncertain.

An unsightly, disturbing flower,

Whose twigs will be reborn as Thorns

Tomorrow and perhaps

I'll be the reason to someone else's love story

<u>Midnight</u>

It's after 12 am

And i'll be your delicate piece of artwork now.

I'll be one of the rusted books

At the corner of the library

Where lovers meet to discover their authenticity.

I'll be the be the pathway of young dreamers

To the flicker of hope where the universe can see me.

Avni Arneja

<u>Poetry</u>

Falling in love before it's time,

Didn't surmise that it would be a crime.

Braids ending in bows,

On pencil-sooted desk,

As we sat appose,

Tale of two- burlesque.

Fingers intertwined,

Behind the stairwell door,

Shelter from the rumored wind,

Pitiful parting as the clock struck four.

Guileful glances,

Secrets typed under the sheets,

Dialing in, awaiting chances,

By the intersecting Streets.

Monisha Raghunath Dasappa

<u>Poetry</u>

Zany humor,
Hard to overlook in a college-fest,
A telenovela kind of blooper,
Put my heart at unrest.
Shared cans of coke,
Inseparable in hallways.
Hanging upon every word spoke,
Promise of together, always.
'Don't look', 'don't talk',
Envy slid in to reign,
Spiralling down,more than one balk,
Dishonored deed in deign.
Much to their chagrin,
Ending right where it did begin.
Conceded defeat,
Swearing not to repeat,
Down the same road,
Couple more times to be sure,
Erring with every code,
Boat sans oar, to the moor.
Melodies of contour,
Ardent accolades to allure.

-Monisha Raghunath Dasappa

<u>When I have chosen him</u>

When I have chosen him,
I become a part of him,
Just like a spark is to the fire,
I lose my identity
And see myself in him,
As my soul merges in his
He is the only source of light,
In my world,
My eyes are forever seeking him,
I sleep to see him in my dreams
The way he smiles at m
That I curse my eye lids
For its blinking becomes a hurdle
For my eyes to drink all his sweetness
He smells in love
He is felt in my heart beats
The vibrations of my universe
Turns peaceful with his presence.
I can never stop telling him
How much I love him
My soul, only knows his face
Every cell of my body echoes his name
He is the passion running in my blood
He is the gem nourishing my soul
He is the reason I feel to breathe
He is the reason I want to live
Just to be his servant
For the rest of my life
Surrendering myself to him forever
To wrap my mind win
The images of his eternal love and care
I feel non-substantial without him
The moment becomes perfect
When I have chosen him.

- Krishna Thankey

<u>When I Pick Myself Up In His Arms</u>
I gaze at him
And he open
The depths of his soul
Leaning my head on his chest
And hearing those heart beat
Echoing my name
My heart only sings
My soul wants to fly with his
How translucent he is,
So pure, so innocent yet so manly
He is my Knight in shining armour
Just disguised in a human body
Radiating the perfect light
So how far can the fire be
Gazing again
I read the stories of his soul
He is magic
Rejuvenating my soul
To another reality
Where it's only he and me

And the cosmic energy
Helping my soul
To mingle with his
His caressing hug
Drenching me with the love
Seeping from every pore of his skin
How fortunate of m
To be his forever
He makes me feel safe being around
He listens my heart out
Even when I don't utter a word
Lusting for his mind
Tasting the depths of love
Through his soul

fall for him day and night
He helps me carve myself better
He magnifies my qualities
And helps my soul to bloom brighter
He is the limitless ocean
Of masculinity and loyalty
He is flawless
Fabulous and forever fruitful.
He is a fighter
and every time a winner
Wearing all the imperfection
Perfectly as gems on invest
le Prince Charming Crown
He takes my heart away
Every time
Just with one delicate gaze
I gradually realised
The love between us is eternal
For whom
I picked myself up in his arms
And for the first time in my life
I felt, I was at the exact spot
At the exact moment
I felt there was
A place for me in the world.

-Krishna Thankey

<u>Letter to my future love...</u>

Hey!

You know what you still make me nervous. Whenever I think about my future with you, it gives me mixed feelings. I have no idea about what destiny have decided for us. I don't know where you are, but still I'm writing this to you.

There is always a phase in everyone life where you meet a person and fall in love. But very few people are lucky enough to meet the right ones. But I am luckier enough to write this to you. May be now you would be with someone else or maybe you would be waiting for me. Loving someone truely is like a magic dream come true. But i loved a wrong one. At this moment I don't want anyone in my life. But I know one day in future ill need someone. Someone who can make me fall in love again. Someone who can make me believe that wrong cannot happen in love everytime. Someone who can fill all my scars, can accept me with all my flaws the way I'm. Someone who is always there to support me, who stands strong beside me like a wind. Someone who never tells me to change for others. Someone who loves my stupid things my idiotic behaviour. Someone who would never leave my hand for someone else. Someone with whom I'll feel safe. Someone who would look into my eyes but it would connect my soul. Someone who would always be my friend first. Someone who makes me the best version of myself. Someone who never breaks be again, because the thought of this makes be more fearful.

People say that if you can love a wrong person so much imagine loving the right one. I have no clue when we'll meet or maybe we have crossed paths. I hope that you never get any heart break, sorrow, sadness in your life. I only hope that because I don't want you to go through any of that with me. I just want to be happy and want to grow with you. I promise that I will love and protect you no matter what. I'll treat your heart as if it were my own. I promise to never break it. I won't ever make you doubt my loyalty or love for you. You will definitely feel it. Because I'm very bad at expressing my feelings but i know when you are there with me everything will be awesome. I promise to treat you like my super hero and always understand you. If sometime we have a fight we will always talk it out. I will always give you, your space and promise to never make you sleep sad. No matter what I'll always do stupid childish things to bring your cute smile on your face. Because I love seeing you smile and for me it is very precious. I know you would be reading this and smiling right now, but keep smiling like that only. It looks super cute on you. I know no relationship is perfect but when we both will be together we will make the best one. At last just wanted to say you be crazy, laugh out loud until your stomach pains and you fall on the ground.

Lastly, I know at the right time, right place we will meet soon. And I can't wait to meet you. Wish the day comes soon. Few lines for you "Jise Dua main maine manga tha

Voh aaj mujhe mil Gaya…

Der se hi sahi par aaj mera

Pyar mukammal ho hi Gaya"…

I'll be waiting sincerely

Your future girl

Shivangi Jaiswal

<u>When it's you!!</u>

You gave me peace,

You shower love and filled every moment with glee...

You took away my darker days,

You took away my pain…

You walked through that storm and even rain...

You made me fall for you even more,

And so I keep my sight just on you and adore…

You the only one with whom I wanna walk every mile,

And you please be the reason I always smile…

You made it possible for me to survive

You the reason why I'm still alive♥

Naureen Rafat

<u>Emotion of being in Love</u>

To be touched by you is likely to have a dream that takes a little too long to make it true...

I sat down calmly and waits for you...

Even my words never reached nor got a glance of you...

Emotions gets fluctuated but they never get to see you…

All can be undertake but for now it can only be waits

To make every desire come true...

Or to be touched by you…

Naureen Rafat

<u>The Right Choice</u>

Life's all about to strive perfection,

Mindfully pick the best perception.

Spend leisure time in self reflection,

Brave step leads to right direction.

Face with courage never fear rejection,

Use opportunity for next better selection.

Speak clear words with no conflection,

Always seek respect not fake attention.

Don't get trapped on physical attraction,

Wrong person forces to beg affection.

Critics are powerless without your reaction,

Choose the one who unravel heart connection.

Care with love without any expectation,

Keep relation safe with full dedication.

Forgive the mistakes provide course correction,

The Right Choice makes happy memories collection.

-Deepti

<u>Hope of Light</u>

When the inner light constantly flicker,

Ability to tolerate things begin splinter.

Time passes memories seem to fade quicker,

Though little happiness makes soul quiver.

Surrender to that which makes heart flutter,

Stand firm then calmly open mind shutter.

Save precious relations clear the clutter,

Spread pure love as bread with butter.

Share every feeling when in fear,

One in a million who got you clear.

No matter true buddy far or near,

But always there to wipe off tear.

Never give up on people who care,

Gift of humanity is found very rare.

Good Karma in life makes better player,

Hope of Light illuminate by silent prayer.

-Deepti

<u>Poetry</u>

याद है जब चूड़ियों वाली अम्मा के चूड़ी पहनाते वक्त

कुछ चूड़ियां मेरे हाथों में धंस गई थी

और उभर गया था वहां एक जख्म

तुमने कितना डांटा था था चूड़ी वाली अम्मा को

और मुझे मलहम लगाते लगाते रो पड़े थे

हां बस वही जख्म मैं आज भी कुरेदती हूं

जब पड़ोस वाली मीना के जन्मदिन पर जाना था

तो मैंने आंखों में काजल लगाया था

याद है तुमने कहा था,

तुम्हारी आंखों में आने पर सुंदर हो जाता है काजल

और मेरे माथे को चूम कर कहीं खो पड़े थे

हां बस वही काजल मैं आज भी लगाती हूं

जब घर में गणपति की पूजा रखी थी

और सभी पड़ोसियों को बुलाया था

तब मैंने पीला सूट पहनकर

माथे पर छोटी सी बिंदी को सजाया था

याद है तुमने कहा था,

तुम्हारे चांद से मुखड़े पर यह बिंदी एक छोटा सा सितारा लग रही है

और मेरे हाथों को थाम कर मेरी गोद में सो पड़े थे||

-Ipsit

Bio

&

Pictures

SASWAT BARAL

Age 20.
From: Rourkela Steel City, Odisha.
Passionate About: Writing, Cricket, Football, Kabbadi&Music.
Role Models: Rahul Dravid, Cristiano Ronaldo
Hobbies: Blogging, Food, Writing

AMAN RAI

IG: aman_rai_forever

Bio: Basically from a small district of Uttar Pradesh, Ballia and proud to belong from the land of Mangal Pandey, Chittu Pandey and Gauri Shankar Rai, itterateur Hazari Prasad Dwivedi and modern saint Bhrigu Maharaj .

MAHENDRA KESHWANI

IG: mahi_s_diary

Bio: MAHENDRA KESHWANI is a passionate writer, a Co-author (You, I and Destiny), a Poet and a Teacher (Maths). He writes his heart out. He is a Freelance writer. Not much of a talker but express his feelings and ideas through his writing. Basically,

VIVEK_JR.

IG: _vivek_jr

Bio: Belong to Bihar, he is a simple and Panglossian person, completed his graduation in English hons. Loves to write his heart out on the paper in leisure.

NILOFAR FAROOQUI TAUSEEF

IG: writernilofar

Bio: Meet our co-author Nilofar Farooqui Tauseef, Basically from Bihar Sharif, Nalanda but staying in Mumbai. She is Software Engineer as her profession and writing poems, ghazals, scripts, quotes, Microtale, is her hobby.

SHOBIT KUMAR

IG: @vajud_ek_safar and @akhil_shobhit_7.0

Bio: Shobhit Kumar is Doing M.sc with chemistry in MNIT Jaipur, Rajasthan. He is basically from Bareilly, Uttar Pradesh. He loves to write poems, quotes and sometimes stories too. He loves photography, travelling and spending time with Nature. He is also an Ex Navodayan i.e. Alumni of JNV Shahjahanpur UP.

SHAZEEN SANIA

IG: @__thoughts_into_words

Hey,this is shazeen sania from Kolkata, a graduate and an aspirant of civil services.In order to express the amalgamation of thoughts and feeling, she pen them down through words.

SWATI BHARADWAJ

IG: swati024

Bio: This is Swati Bharadwaj, belong to UP (Muzaffarnagar), currently living in Silicon Valley of India, Bangalore. She is so much in love with movies as well as dogs. Working as 3D animator, she is fond of writing her heart out. Talented dancer who is always available for her friend

ARPAN VINEET LAKRA
IG: everything_is_here_now_
Bio: Hey, there. I am an entrepreneur in the travel innovation space and a somewhat decent cook, from Bokaro Steel City.

NEMIKA SHARMA

IG: author_nemikasharma

Bio: Nemika Sharma is a gladsome and lightsome soul.A poetess with her debut poetry book ''thoughts that breath''.she is fierce and love to pen down emotion, A firm believer of god and true love, who personally presumes that love has strongest and purest vibes in it.

TARUN JEEVNANI
IG: tarun.jeevan
Engineer by profession, runs a family business but his heart and mind still wander through mysterious paths in search for his goal. Good at coding and knowledgeable enough to keep you at your wits.

KSHAMA

IG: Kshama1_

Bio: Kshama has written and published ten books. She has won the Literoma achiever's award.

SARTHAK LAKHANI
IG: _.the_genius._
Bio: He is an eighteen year old boy pursuing engineering. He is from Bhopal (M.P) who started penning in 2018 and his future goal is to be an Entrepreneur. His interests and hobbies are travelling, food blogging and writing. He is straight forward, confident and have an optimistic attitude.

MOHIT BIRLA
IG: birla584
Bio: Myself Mohit Birla. By Profession;   I am a student and pursuing my Btech in mechanical Branch from Rayat Institute of engineering and information technology (Rupnagar) (Punjab). And similarly! I have done; my schooling from Shiwalik public school Rupnagar (Punjab)

PRINCE THAKUR

IG: thakurprince7001.
Meet with the your co-author Mr prince thakur, from azamgarh UP.he is student from profession and is fond of reeding poem ,and sayari.he want to tell you about a love story

NIKITA MALIK

IG: nikitamalikwrites
Bio: COFFEE QUEEN °~° WRITER °~°
NOCTURNAL °~° READING

KSHITIJ ANAND

IG: kshitij_anand

Bio: From Gorakhpur (UP) but currently lives in
Bhubneshwar. And his Hobbies are Freelance
content writer and web designer.

DEEPTI LAKRA

IG: Deeptilakra

Bio: Have done my graduation from Delhi
University in history and currently pursuing my
diploma in teaching. And I am from dilwalon ki
Dilli.

SNEH ANTIL

IG: Weavingofwords

Bio: Sneh Antil, a student pursuing MCA who loves to weave feelings into words. Writing is not just a passion, but a therapy which made her realize the power of words when framed beautifully. She's all about untamed hopes, searching eyes and a soul in a mess revealing herself layer by layer.

Bushra Shaikh (Saeraa.S)

IG: the.soultalks

Bio: Saeraa. S is her pen name, lives in Pune and is currently pursuing degree in Mechanical Engineering. She's an animal lover, likes to read suspense and write on philosophy. Her interests is to study animal psychology. Night sky and nature are her inspiration. Believes in karma.

VAIDEHI KATHOTE
Bio: Medical student.

SHALINI TOPPO

IG: emotion.labile

Bio: Shalini is a doctor, an amicable fellow who has uncovered her muse for writing. Though the words were always her friend yet it took her time to understand this calling. Alongside writingyou can often find her painting illustration, drawing or at time just being behind thecamera lens trying to capture the nature at its best.

ADITI NAYAK

IG: aditi_beyond_words

Bio: I am Aditi Nayak, a girl full of surprises and dreams. I love to spend time with the nature and animals. I am a 1st year graduating student in the Ravenshaw University.

KARTIK POWAR

IG: dust_n_memories

SANDESHPATAIHE

IG: true_word_voice

Bio: I'm from city of Rice GONDIA, Maharashtra. I'm a professional teacher at a Computer Institute and love to write about Social, Inspirational, Emotional and other genres. I also like to play Guitar, Dance and participate in Dramas. My Dream is to make the world a happy place.

SHILPA KRISHNA

IG: @thesoulbite.

Bio: Shilpa Krishna is an experienced content writer and a former sub-editor, who quit her job as a software engineer to pursue her passion for writing. She writes about everything, be it love, sports, technology, bikes, cars, or marketing. Apart from writing, she loves reading and travelling. Follow her on instagram at @thesoulbite.

JASPREET KAUR

IG: _kaur_jaspreet_

Bio: This is Jaspreet Kaur. I have done masters in mathematics. I have keen interest in writing poetry,

motivational content etc

VIKRANT MOHRIR

Bio: Is a Medical student and a novels lover. His journey from one sided lover to getting his 'dream girl' clearly reflects in his write-up. His struggle and love for her is highlighted in poems & writings.

NIKHIL TIWARI

IG: _nikhiltiwari

Bio: Guy from "dilli-dil valon ki", an introvert for self but unexpectedly friendly by nature, is named Nikhil (the one without boundaries). He graduated from Jamia University, has deep love for physics

AVNI ARNEJAA

Bio: Young dreamer and writer

NAUREEN RAFAT

IG: _crooked_corner

Bio: She is simple yet quirky kinda girl with many dreams beneath her eyes. An easy-going person with a positive attitude towards life. She was born on 4th March, hailing from Aurangabad, Maharashtra .She's been in teaching profession since past few years.She's very much fond of kids and of course an animal lover too including only Cats and kittens in her list.

SHIVANGI JAISWAL

Bio: She is from kolkata. She is doing her post graduation in finance. A writer by day and a reader by night. She loves to bring smiles and hapiness to many faces, so she is into socialservice. She thinks "Every story is unique so embrace yourself to the best"

KRISHNA THANKEY

She is Krishna Thankey, an Indian, exploring English Literature. Being an ambivert, she hascreated her own flawless world. She initiated fabricating poetries to bring out the passion of writing that she has been holding within herself for a long time

MONISHA RAGHUNATH DASAPPA

This is MonishaRaghunathDasappa, hailing from Bangalore. Twenty something doctor to be and a poet at heart. Would like to augment her writing enough to call herself Ms. Caroline Rozario'sprotege, someday.Writing, more of poetry and less of prose has always been her refuge. From pepping boring classes with rhyme to pouring out what weighed her heart down..

DEEPTI

I am Deepti (Owner of business Rvjd Creations, Artist and Poetess). I love to convey my feelings and share my experiences to inspire others through my self made bilingual poems. I always try to indulge in things that keeps me motivated, happy and satisfied.

IPSITI PANDEY

I am a 17 year old and I am Class 12th Student. I am from Azamgarh Uttar Pradesh (UP).

9 789389 923056